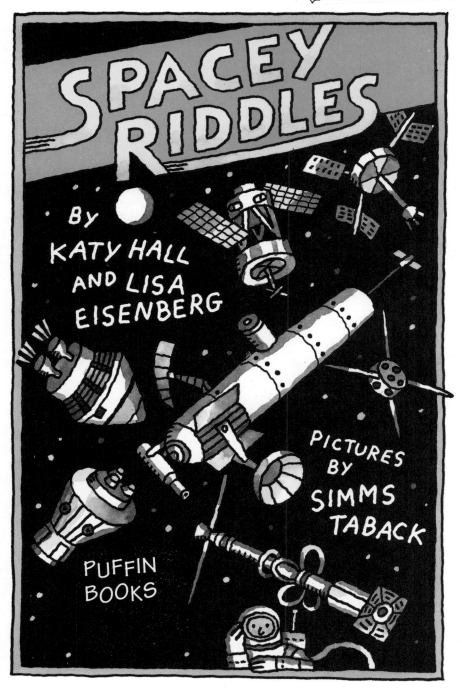

SPACEY RIDDLES

BY
KATY HALL
AND LISA
EISENBERG

PICTURES
BY
SIMMS
TABACK

PUFFIN
BOOKS

PUFFIN BOOKS
Published by the Penguin Group
Penguin Books USA Inc., 375 Hudson Street, New York, New York 10014, U.S.A.
Penguin Books Ltd, 27 Wrights Lane, London W8 5TZ, England
Penguin Books Australia Ltd, Ringwood, Victoria, Australia
Penguin Books Canada Ltd, 10 Alcorn Avenue, Toronto, Ontario, Canada M4V 3B2
Penguin Books (N.Z.) Ltd, 182-190 Wairau Road, Auckland 10, New Zealand

Penguin Books Ltd, Registered Offices: Harmondsworth, Middlesex, England

First published in the United States of America by Dial Books for Young Readers,
a division of Penguin Books USA Inc., 1992
Published in a Puffin Easy-to-Read edition, 1995

1 3 5 7 9 10 8 6 4 2

Text copyright © Katy Hall and Lisa Eisenberg, 1992
Illustrations copyright © Simms Taback, 1992
All rights reserved

THE LIBRARY OF CONGRESS HAS CATALOGED THE DIAL BOOKS EDITION AS FOLLOWS:
Hall, Katy.
Spacey riddles / by Katy Hall and Lisa Eisenberg; pictures by Simms Taback.
p. cm.
Summary: Riddles about the sun, stars, moon, planets, and space travel.
ISBN 0-8037-0814-9 ISBN 0-8037-0815-7 (lib. bdg.)
1. Riddles, Juvenile. 2. Outer space—Juvenile humor.
[1. Outer space—Wit and humor. 2. Riddles.] I. Eisenberg, Lisa. II. Taback, Simms, ill.
III. Title.
PN6371.5.H37 1992 818'.5402—dc20 90-42508 CIP AC

Puffin Books ISBN 0-14-037385-3

Puffin® and Easy-to-Read® are registered trademarks of Penguin Books USA Inc.
Printed in the United States of America

Reading Level 1.9

What holds the sun up?

Sun beams.

What would you get
if you crossed a comet
with a guppy?

A starfish.

What kind of bulbs should
you plant on the moon?

Light bulbs!

What is the astronaut's favorite meal?

Launch!

How would you recognize
an elephant on the moon?

By the big E on its space suit!

What do you call
a crazy spaceman?

An astro-nut.

If an athlete gets athlete's foot, what does an astronaut get?

Missile toe.

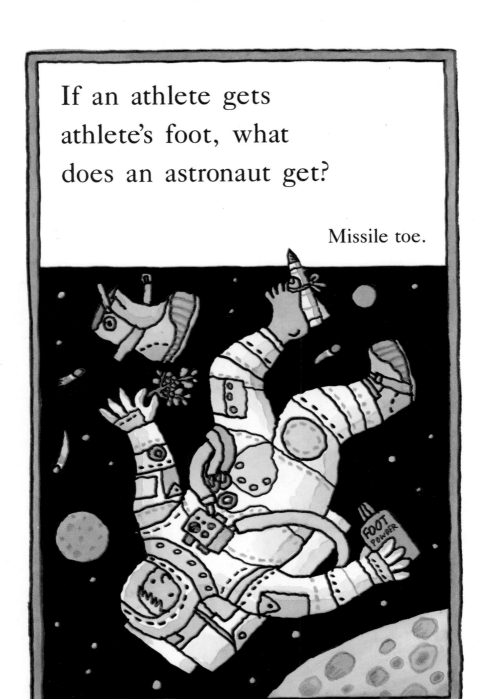

How many balls of string
would it take
to reach the moon?

Just one—a *very* big one!

Who was the first person
in space?

The man in the moon.

When is a window like a star?

When it's a skylight.

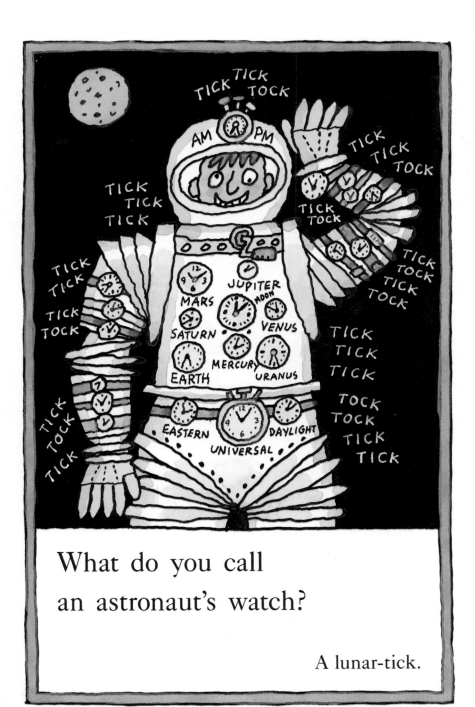

What do you call
an astronaut's watch?

A lunar-tick.

Which is heavier,
a half moon or a full moon?

A half moon,
because a full moon is lighter.

What did the boy star
say to the girl star?

I really glow for you!

Why was the baby constellation sillier than the daddy constellation?

Because he was a little dippier!

What kind of light
goes around the earth?

A satel-lite!

What kind of songs
do planets like to sing?

Nep-tunes!

Why did the two stars get married?

They took a shine to each other!

What poem can you find
in outer space?

A uni-verse!

Why couldn't the astronaut
land on the moon?

It was already full.

What did the astronaut
cook for lunch?

An unidentified frying object.

Why did the astronaut
take a nap so close
to the sun?

She was a light sleeper!

What kind of star
wears sunglasses?

A movie star!

What's big and bright
and silly?

A fool moon.

Why is the North Star
the smartest star?

Because it's the brightest!

What kind of bath
can you take in outer space?

A sun bath!

Why did the astronaut
move to Saturn?

He heard it was out of this world!

What did the big rocket
say to the little rocket?

Take off, kid!

How did the astronaut
serve dinner in outer space?

On flying saucers.

And how did the astronaut serve drinks?

In sun glasses!

What kind of jacket
would you wear on the sun?

A blazer!

Where does a witch keep her spaceship?

In the broom closet.

What did Saturn
say to Jupiter?

Don't call me—
I'll give you a ring!

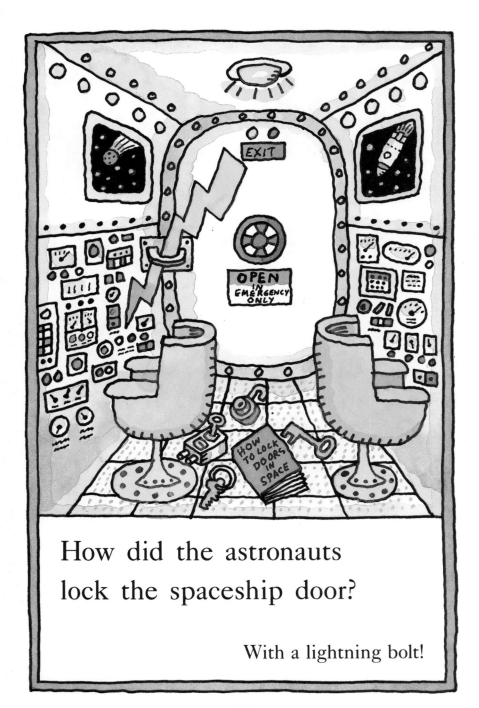

How did the astronauts
lock the spaceship door?

With a lightning bolt!

What's the best way
to talk to a martian?

Long distance!

How did the sailor know
there wasn't
a man in the moon?

He'd been to sea.

41

Why is a cloud like Santa Claus?

Because it holds the rain, dear!

What's soft and white
and comes from Mars?

A Mars-mallow!

What did the moon
say to the star?

Boy, are you far-out!

What should an astronaut
watch when walking on
the outside of his spaceship?

His step.

What baseball game might
be played in outer space?

The Astros versus the Angels!

What's a martian's
normal eyesight?

20-20-20!

Where should a 300-pound
space alien go?

On a diet.